Peppa Pig™

D0549793

Peppa's First Glasses

Peppa and George are outside playing with their friend Pedro Pony. They are busy jumping in muddy puddles. Splash! Splosh! Splish!
"Ha! Ha! Ha!" Peppa giggles as she jumps up and down.

Splosh!

Splash!

"Argh! Ooh!" Pedro exclaims as he slips in a puddle and falls over. His glasses fly high into the air and land on the grass.

"Neigh! Where are my glasses?" Pedro asks Peppa and George, stumbling about. Pedro can't see very well without them.

Neigh!

Peppa and George look for Pedro's glasses. George quickly finds them and tries them on. "Silly George!" Peppa says. She takes the glasses and gives them back to Pedro. "Here they are." "Thank you," says Pedro as he puts them on.

"Pedro, why do you wear glasses?" Peppa asks.
"I need to," replies Pedro. "My daddy says so.
He's an optician."

"What's an optician?" Peppa wonders. Pedro explains. "An optician checks that you can see clearly. He does an eye test."

"Shall I give you an eye test?" Pedro asks Peppa.
Peppa agrees, and Pedro leans in close.

Snort!
Snort!

"Hmmm, interesting," he says, rubbing his chin.
"Close one eye and say what you can see."
"I can see George," Peppa says. George snorts.

"Now, close both eyes," Pedro instructs Peppa.
Peppa closes both her eyes.
"I can't see anything," Peppa says.
"Hmmm, can't see anything. Very, very
interesting . . ." Pedro says.
"I think you need glasses!"

Soon it is Pedro's home time.
He waves goodbye to his
friends and goes home
with his mum.

Peppa and George go inside.
"Pedro gave me an eye test and I need glasses," says Peppa. "When I closed my eyes, I couldn't see anything."

"No one can see anything with their eyes closed," Mummy Pig explains.

"But . . ." Peppa sighs. ". . . Pedro knows all about glasses." "All right, Peppa," chuckles Daddy Pig. "Let's take you to the optician for a proper eye test."

Peppa and Mummy Pig are at the optician's.
"What can I do for you?" Mr Pony asks Peppa.

"I need an eye test, please," Peppa replies, jumping up into his special chair. "Of course," Mr Pony says. "Put these special glasses on and then look at the chart." Mr Pony is going to test Peppa's eyes.

"Can you read these for me,
please?" asks Mr Pony, pointing
at some numbers.
Peppa says what she sees:
"1, 2, 3, 4, 5, 6, 7, 8!"
"Very good," Mr Pony says.
"And now these colours, please."
"Red, orange, blue, green,
yellow, purple!" says Peppa.
"Excellent!" Mr Pony says.

Mummy Pig helps Peppa try on some glasses
while Mr Pony checks the test results.
Some pairs look a little funny!

"How about these?" Mummy Pig says to Peppa holding
out some red, heart-shaped glasses.
"Wow! I like these ones, Mummy," says Peppa.
They both agree that Peppa looks fantastic in the glasses.

Mr Pony comes back with the results.
"Good news: Peppa has perfect eyesight!"
"Oh! So I don't need glasses." Peppa sighs disappointedly.
"But I really wanted some."

"Oh," Mr Pony says, thinking. "I suppose you could have some sunglasses."
Peppa puts on a pair of red, heart-shaped sunglasses.
"Fantastic!" Peppa says. "I hope it's sunny every day so I can always wear them!"